W9-BPL-357

St. Croix Falls
Public Library

It's Time for School, Stinky Face

By Lisa McCourt

Illustrated by Cyd Moore

Troll

BridgeWater Books

Text copyright © 2000 by Lisa McCourt.
Illustrations copyright © 2000 by Cyd Moore.

Published by BridgeWater Books, an imprint and registered trademark
of Troll Communications L.L.C.

All rights reserved. No part of this book may be reproduced or utilized in
any form or by any means, electronic or mechanical, including photocopying,
recording, or by any information storage and retrieval system, without written
permission from the publisher.

Produced by Boingo Books, Inc.

Printed in Singapore.

10 9 8 7 6 5 4 3 2 1

"It's almost time for school, Stinky Face," said Mama as she packed my lunch.
But I had a question.

Mama, what if the school bus was already stuffed with too many kids and the second I stepped inside, all the tires popped flat?

"If all the tires popped flat, I'd call the circus. I'd ask the clowns to come and drive you and the other kids to school in their crazy little cars."

But, Mama, what if I was so dizzy from the crazy clown car ride that I got lost

at school and ended up in the principal's office instead of my classroom?

"If that happened, the principal would help you find your class."

But what if she's really a **WITCH** just pretending to be the principal?

"If the witch did that, I'd come and get you. I'd feed you raspberries while I sang 'Skip to My Lou' and spun you around forty-seven times with a teacup on your head.

my darling!

"That's the secret formula for breaking all nasty spells. I learned it in Girl Scouts. Then I'd help you find your classroom."

But, Mama, what if the glue had spilled at art time ~ buckets and buckets of it ~ and the door to my classroom had gotten stuck

"If you couldn't budge that door, I'd get you the biggest, bounciest pogo stick ever so you could

Boing Boing Boing

right up to your classroom window and land inside."

But, Mama, what if I accidentally bounced right and made all her pencils fall and onto Ms. Ritter's desk everybody laughed?

"Oooo, if you did that, you'd have to pick up all the pencils and tell Ms. Ritter you were sorry."

But, Mama, what if Ms. Ritter laughed herself silly and instead of teaching us our letters and numbers, she taught us how to make armpit noises and dance the

hokey~ pokey?

...you put your left side in put your left side in a You do the hoke turn yourself around...

ke your left side out
ake it all about...
okey and you

"If that happened, you
would have an interesting
day at school!"

But, Mama, what if it was my turn to feed the class fish? Only when I went to the aquarium, the fish were all wearing itsy-bitsy sunglasses and drinking little milkshakes through teeny-tiny straws?

"They wouldn't be very hungry if they were all filled up on milkshakes! But Ms. Ritter would probably give you another turn soon."

And then, Mama, what if we were playing on the playground and an alien spaceship landed right next to the jungle gym? What if the aliens liked to play catch with mudpies made of slimy green alien goop and whenever you caught one it went Splat all over you and you were slimed?

"If that happened, you would have a messy day, but a fun one too, I bet!"

Mama, what if we walked in two straight lines back into our classroom, only when we got there, all the desks were flying around in the air?

"If your desks were flying, I bet you would all hop right onto them and have a zoomy game of desk-tag."

But, Mama, what if it was circle time?

"Oh, well, if it was circle time, I'm sure all the desks would park themselves in their neat rows so that you could get out of them and sit in your circle."

But, Mama, what if it was storytime circle time, only Ms. Ritter forgot all her stories and she made me tell a story to the class instead?

"You know what, my little Stinky Face?"

What, Mama?

"I think you'd do just fine."

St. Croix Falls
Public Library